Smiley's Christmas Eve

PJ Hawkins

NEWMAN SPRINGS PUBLISHING
320 Broad Street
Red Bank, NJ 07701

First originally published by Newman Springs Publishing 2021

ISBN 978-1-63692-264-5 (Paperback)
ISBN 978-1-63692-265-2 (Hardcover)
ISBN 978-1-63692-266-9 (Digital)

Printed in the United States of America

To Eddie. Never stop writing.

It was Christmas Eve at the North Pole. A fresh layer of snow covered the ground. The air was crisp and cold, and the stars twinkled above with excitement. The elves had been hard at work all year making bats, balls, games, dolls, and many other kinds of toys. Now the time had come to get them packed and ready for the big trip with Santa.

Smiley sat patiently waiting, holding her breath with the rest of the toys, waiting and wondering if she would be on Santa's list this year. Smiley was a rag doll made from scraps of cloth stuffed with bits of foam. She didn't look at all like the other dolls. Her hair was made from short stubby pieces of leftover yarn. The foam stuffing poked out in the most peculiar places and made her appear quite lumpy. Her dress was a patchwork of bits and pieces of multicolored fabric from the scrap box. A beautiful big smile had been carefully stitched on her face. But Smiley was not happy. She felt alone and sad. What if no one wanted a rag doll this year?

Doesn't anyone play with rag dolls anymore? Smiley thought to herself.

Santa put on his spectacles, leaned back in his rocker, and unrolled a very long wish list. After giving thoughtful consideration to each request, he selected just the right toy for each girl and boy. The workshop was silent. All the toys held their breath, hoping they would be on Santa's list. For twelve long months, they had dreamed of the Christmas Eve ride from house to house in Santa's bright-red sleigh. They wanted so much to hear the jingle of sleigh bells and feel the cold wind blowing around them. But more than anything, they wanted to see the delight on the faces of the children as they opened their presents on Christmas morning.

Some of the toys had spent all year at the workshop because they had not been on Santa's wish list last year. They had been given chores to do and, throughout the year, had helped Santa and his elves prepare for this Christmas. The work was not hard. In fact, it was even fun most of the time. Still, it was the dream of every toy to find a home of their very own someday.

A home of my own, thought Smiley. Oh how I would love to have my very own special place. Someone to sing and laugh with, a place with my very own friend to share my dreams. Smiley had spent the last two years around the workshop, and while she enjoyed working with Santa and his elves, she still dreamed of finding that special someone to call her own.

Only a few toys remained as Santa neared the end of his list. Then it happened. Smiley heard those dreaded words once again.

"Well, that's all for this year," said Santa as he leaned forward in his rocker and took off his spectacles. "Pack it up. Don't forget to pack a few extra bears. You never know when they'll be needed." With just a few more hours until Christmas Eve, everyone must work hard to have everything ready to go on time.

Smiley felt as if her heart would break. She blinked back a tear that was trying very hard to make its way down her cheek. Think happy thoughts, she said to herself. This always seemed to work before when she had been disappointed. Smiley knew all those not going on the sleigh would now be given chores. She couldn't cry now! She just couldn't let Santa see a tearstain on her face. She wanted to look her best for him. At that very moment, Santa called her name.

"Smiley," said Santa, "you will be in charge of seeing to it that all the dolls going with me have all their belongings with them. It's a big job. Can you handle it?"

"Yes," Smiley said in her bravest voice. For the moment, her disappointment seemed to disappear. The smile that had been stitched on her face seemed to glow and brighten her whole face. She felt proud that Santa had given her such an important job.

"Smiley," called Santa.

There was a short pause. For a brief moment, Smiley's heart seemed to stop beating. What could it be? What was on his mind?

"You helped me last year, didn't you?" he asked.

With a sigh of relief, Smiley quickly replied, "Yes, I did."

"Then I'm sure you'll do a fine job again," he said.

"What a beautiful smile," Smiley heard him say as he turned to walk away.

Smiley went to work right away carefully collecting the belongings of each doll, making sure nothing was left behind. Just as she was getting started, she heard a cheerful little voice call to her.

"Hello! My name is Elizabeth. Santa asked me to be your helper."

When Smiley looked up, she could not believe her eyes. Standing in front of her was the most beautiful china doll she had ever seen. Her black hair was as shiny as silk. It was twisted up in the back and held into place by a pearl-covered clip. Her dress was made of powder-blue-colored satin trimmed with strands of pearls. Her china cheeks blushed a soft pink, and her lips glistened a bright rose to match the polish on her nails.

How is it that no one wanted her? thought Smiley. She is so perfect. Surely this must be a mistake. And how was it that she could be so happy about not being on Santa's list?

"Elizabeth," Smiley said. Smiley thought Elizabeth was a beautiful name. It sounded so royal.

"How could someone so beautiful not be on Santa's list?" asked Smiley kindly.

"No one asks for China dolls anymore," Elizabeth replied.

"Doesn't that make you feel sad?" Smiley asked.

"Oh no, not at all. Actually, I was hoping that I wouldn't be on Santa's list. I would love more than anything to go on the sleigh ride with Santa, but this is where I want to stay."

"I don't understand," said Smiley with a puzzled look. "Don't you want someone of your very own to share your dreams with?"

"Yes," replied Elizabeth. "That is exactly what I want, but that is not what happens to china dolls. We are fragile and expensive. No one ever plays with us. They say nice things about us and sit us on a shelf or bed for people to look at. Imagine spending every day just sitting! That is definitely not the life for me!"

And with that said, they went to work. Baby Amaya needed her bottle, two diapers, a bib, and her pacifier. Sophia needed her laptop. Miguel had to have his scooter, and Quinton, his apron and chef's hat. On and on they worked until the last doll had been packed. With a sigh of relief, the girls decided to rest a bit. They plopped down in the chairs that surrounded a small table in the corner of the room. They had finished their work with time to spare. What should they do?

"We should have a tea party," said Smiley.

"What a splendid idea," said Elizabeth, "but we don't have a tea set."

Smiley tiptoed over to a tall cabinet that stood in the corner of the workshop. She carefully opened the doors. On the bottom shelf was a china teapot with two cups and saucers sitting on a beautiful matching serving tray.

"Where did you get that?" exclaimed Elizabeth. "It's beautiful!"

"One day while I was helping the elves, I found it in the pile of broken toys," said Smiley. "Two of the cups were chipped and the saucers cracked. The broken pieces had to be discarded, but the elves gave the rest to me. I always hoped the day would come when I would have someone to share it with."

"And...I have two silk handkerchiefs that we can use for napkins. Let the party begin," said Elizabeth excitedly.

And so it did. They talked and laughed, pretending to be royal guests at the queen's castle.

"One lump or two?" asked Elizabeth as she pretended to offer Smiley the sugar.

"Oh no, thank you, dear. I have quite enough lumps already," replied Smiley, pointing to the lumps of foam sticking out of her arm.

Elizabeth laughed so hard she almost fell out of her chair.

"Oh no!" said Elizabeth. "I mustn't laugh so hard or I shall break into pieces."

They danced around the workshop singing to the top of their lungs.

Suddenly, the door opened. Smiley and Elizabeth stopped their singing and quickly turned to see who was at the door. It was Santa! They were having such fun they had completely forgotten about the time. Night had come, and it was time for Santa to be on his way. Santa had returned to the workshop for his spectacles. As he approached the door, he heard the singing and laughter.

"What a jolly good sound. Don't stop on my account," said Santa with a chuckle. He crossed the room and collected his spectacles from the table. "Could I interest you girls in a sleigh ride tonight?" asked Santa. "The trip is long and cold. It would be so nice to have some music to keep my spirits high."

Smiley and Elizabeth could not believe their ears. This was a dream come true. Of course they wanted to go! They each tried to speak, but no words would come. Instead, they just stood, nodding their heads.

"Is that a yes?" Santa asked.

"Yes!" They both finally got the word out. They were so excited they jumped up and down as if they had springs on their feet.

"Come, we must hurry," Santa said as he bundled them in blankets to keep them warm. All night they sat beside Santa. From rooftop to rooftop, they sang. Santa even joined in on occasion.

It was just before dawn, and Santa was making his last stop. Elizabeth was snuggled in her warm blanket fast asleep.

"Well, this is our last stop," said Santa. He glanced over at Elizabeth soundly sleeping and chuckled. "It looks like it's just the two of us from here on out. Would you like to go down the chimney with me?" he asked. Smiley's eyes twinkled with excitement. Her smile brightened.

"Yes," she replied.

Santa tucked her in his pack, and down they went. The landing was a little bumpy, and since Smiley was in Santa's pack, she could not see. But as soon as they were inside, Santa opened his pack and lifted her out. Smiley gasped as she looked around at the beautiful house. The tree was so big and was decorated to perfection. On a table beside the tree sat a plate with two cookies and a glass of milk.

There was an envelope leaning against the glass of milk. In it was a note to Santa. Santa gave Smiley the milk and cookies. Then he carefully opened the envelope and began to read the note. It said:

> Dear Santa, I am sorry you did not get my wish list this year. Mommy forgot to mail it. I know this is short notice, but if you could leave me something tonight, I would be so happy. Love, Zoe

Santa looked in his pack and saw the extra bears that had been packed. He started to reach for one, then stopped. He remembered hearing Smiley talking to one of the elves one day about wanting a home of her own.

"Smiley," said Santa, "would you like to stay? I know how much you have dreamed of having a home of your own. Zoe is a very good little girl, and this is a beautiful place," he added.

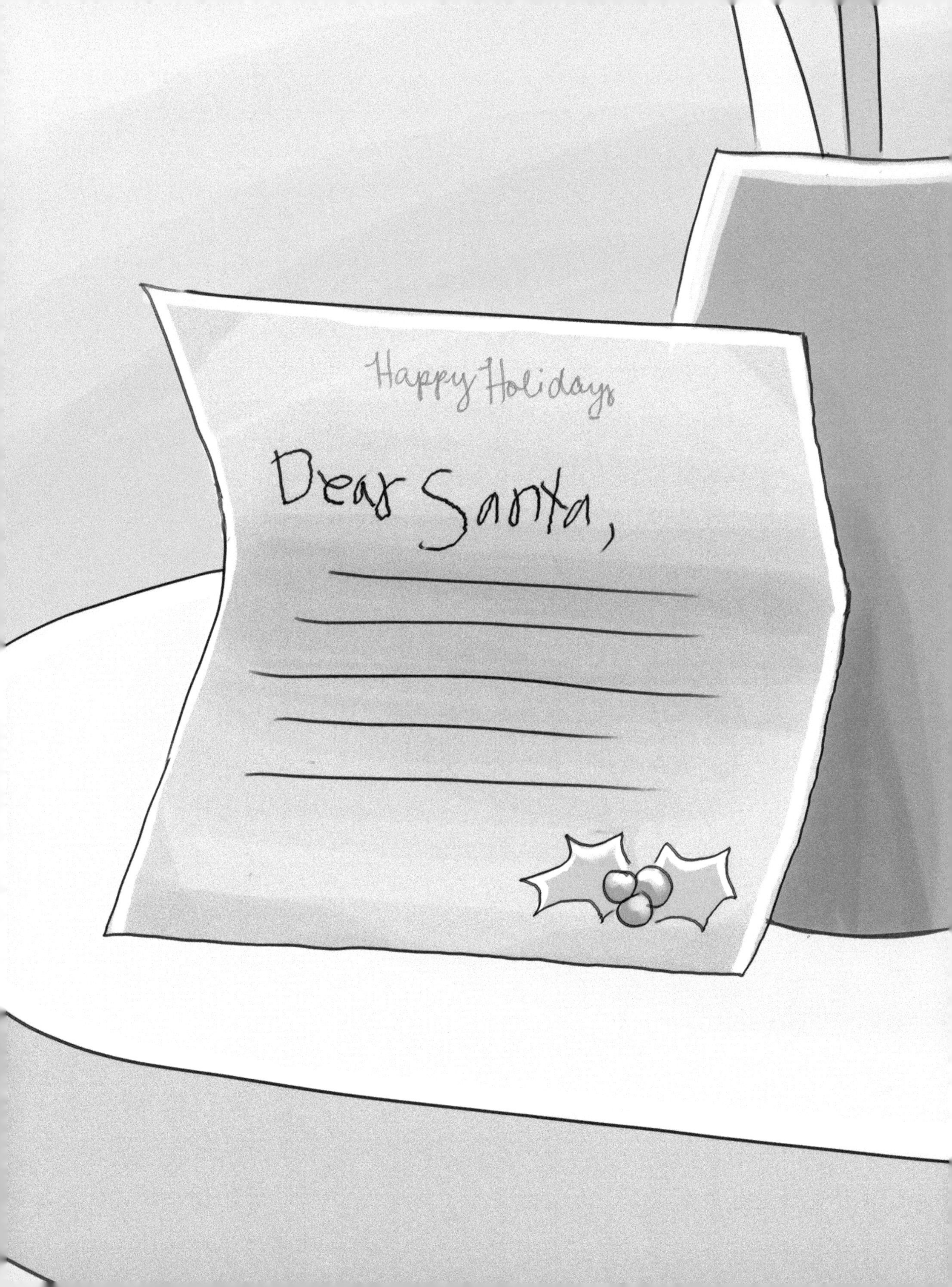
Happy Holidays
Dear Santa,

Smiley didn't know what to say. Santa was right. She had always said she wanted a home of her own. Her heart began to race. She felt as if she could hardly breath. She should be so happy, but instead, she felt confused. This seemed so sudden. Things were different for her now. There was her new friend Elizabeth, and she enjoyed so much the time they spent together. And what about all the work she helped with at the workshop all year long? Who would help if she were to leave? And what about Santa? She was the only one left to keep him company on his ride back home.

Home, thought Smiley. The word seemed to shout at her. She paused for a minute to ponder the thought. I have had a home all along. I already have my own special place. She was so caught up in her thoughts she hardly heard Santa.

"It's up to you," he said.

"I can't stay," said Smiley. "I already have a home!"

"You are absolutely right," said Santa, and he reached into his pack, took out one of the bears, and placed it under the tree for Zoe. He bent down and gently scooped Smiley up in his arms.

"Let's go home!" he said. And up the chimney they went. They climbed into his sleigh, and as they flew away, he gave a gleeful shout. "Ho! Ho! Ho! Merry Christmas!"

The End

26